For my sister Pam, with love
~ P B

For Ravi, Patrycja and
Mehrdad, with love ~ B C

LITTLE TIGER PRESS
An imprint of Magi Publications
1 The Coda Centre, 189 Munster Road, London SW6 6AW
www.littletigerpress.com

First published in Great Britain 2006
This edition published 2007

Text copyright © Paul Bright 2006 • Illustrations copyright © Ben Cort 2006
Paul Bright and Ben Cort have asserted their rights to be identified as the author and illustrator
of this work under the Copyright, Designs and Patents Act, 1988 • All rights reserved
ISBN 978-1-84506-370-2
A CIP catalogue record for this book is available from the British Library

Printed in Singapore by Tien Wah Press Pte.

1 3 5 7 9 10 8 6 4 2

Paul Bright   Ben Cort

I'm Not Going Out There!

LITTLE TIGER PRESS
London

I'm underneath the bed,
Hardly poking out my head.
It's a squeeze and hurts my knees,
but I don't care.
Can you guess, do you know,
Why I whisper soft and low?

I'M
NOT
GOING
OUT
THERE!

There's a dragon breathing smoke,
Who looks far too fierce to stroke,
And his eyes have got a scary sort of stare.
I hope he doesn't stay,
But he's not what makes me say,

I'M NOT GOING OUT THERE!

There's a ghost who's got no head,
With some toast and chocolate spread,
Which I'm sure he would be very
pleased to share.
And though I'd like a bite,
Still I'm keeping out of sight.

I'M NOT GOING OUT THERE!

There are witches, old and stubbly,
Round a bath all hot and bubbly,
Busy washing all their dirty underwear,
Hanging knickers out to dry,
But they're not the reason why

I'M NOT GOING OUT THERE!

There are monsters of all sizes,
Doing ballet exercises,
Wearing tutus, with pink ribbons in their hair.
And though they look quite charming,
There is something else alarming.

I'M NOT GOING

OUT THERE!

Then there's suddenly a shrieking
And a squealing and a squeaking,
Loud enough to give the boldest beast
a scare.
Now I'm shaking and I'm quaking,
There's a noise of something breaking.

I'M NOT GOING OUT THERE!

The dragon turns quite pale,
From his nostrils to his tail,
Feels a trembling in his tum:
"Oh, I really want my mum!"
"Mustn't panic!" gasps the ghost.
"Keep your head! Don't lose your toast!
I can haunt some other day,
Now I need to get away!"

The witches spill their washing
And go splishing, splashing, sploshing,
Soaked and soapy, slipping, sliding,
Searching for a place to hide in.
Hide from what? They'll soon find out!
They can hear it scream and shout,
And it doesn't sound like fun.
Better hurry! Better run!

The monsters don't feel brave,
But they know how to behave,
So they dance off in a row,
Each one on his tippy-toe.

Then all that I can hear,
Very loud and very near,
Is the thing that made them flee.
Do you know what it could be?

It's got teeth that can gnash,
It's got eyes that can flash,
I can hear it grumping, jumping,
Hear it stamping, stomping, thumping.
It's got hands that can snatch,
It's got nails that can scratch.
And it's ready for a fight,
So we're squeezed and squashed up tight!

There it is – my sister Kate!
And she's in a frightful state,
Making shrieking sounds
and leaping in the air.
By now she must know who
Put the spider in her shoe . . .

. . . I'M NOT GOING OUT THERE!